TRAGEDY FROM THE SEA

The Galveston Hurricane of 1900

Bonnie Highsmith Taylor

Perfection Learning®

Illustrations: Sue Cornelison

ABOUT THE AUTHOR

Bonnie Highsmith Taylor is a native Oregonian. She loves camping in the Oregon mountains and watching birds and other wildlife. Writing is Ms. Taylor's first love. But she also enjoys going to plays and concerts, collecting antique dolls, and listening to good music.

Ms. Taylor is the author of several Animal Adventures books, including *Lucy: A Virginia Opossum* and *Zelda: A Little Brown Bat*. She has also written novels, including *Gypsy in the Cellar* and *Kodi's Mare*.

Image Credits: ArtToday (www.arttoday.com) pp. 7, 49; Library of Congress p. 22; NOAA pp. 16, 26, 52; Rosenberg Library, Galveston, Texas, cover, pp. 3, 47, 50

Printed in the United States of America.

For information, contact
Perfection Learning® Corporation
1000 North Second Avenue, P.O. Box 500,
Logan, Iowa 51546-0500.
Phone: 1-800-831-4190 • Fax: 1-712-644-2392
perfectionlearning.com

Paperback ISBN 0-7891-5556-7
Cover Craft® ISBN 0-7569-0662-8

2 3 4 5 6 7 PP 09 08 07 06 05 04

TABLE OF CONTENTS

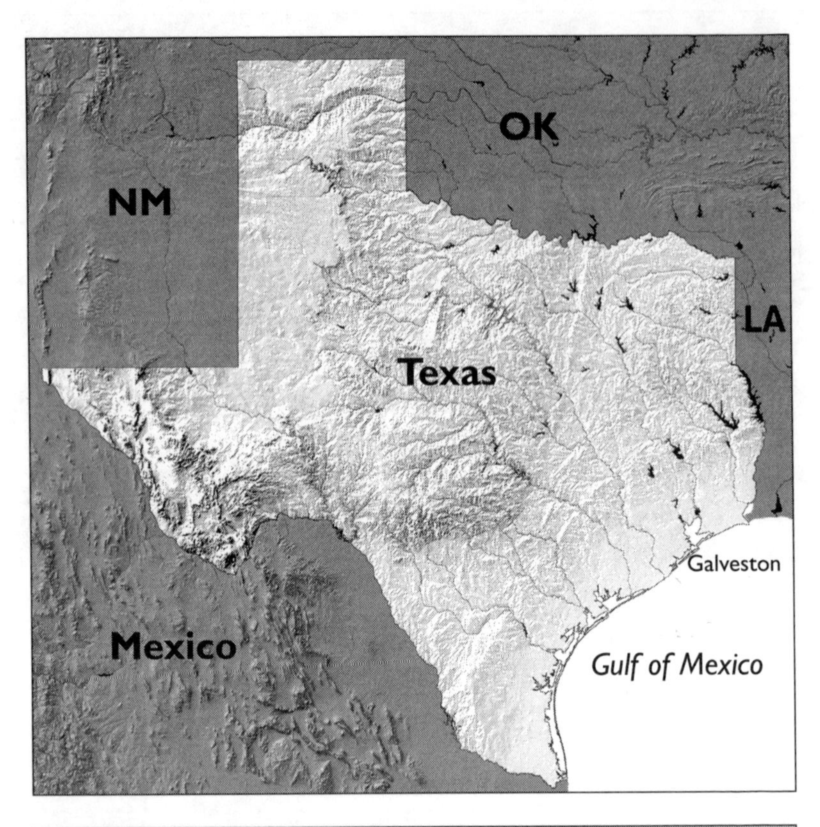
OK
NM
LA
Texas
Galveston
Mexico
Gulf of Mexico

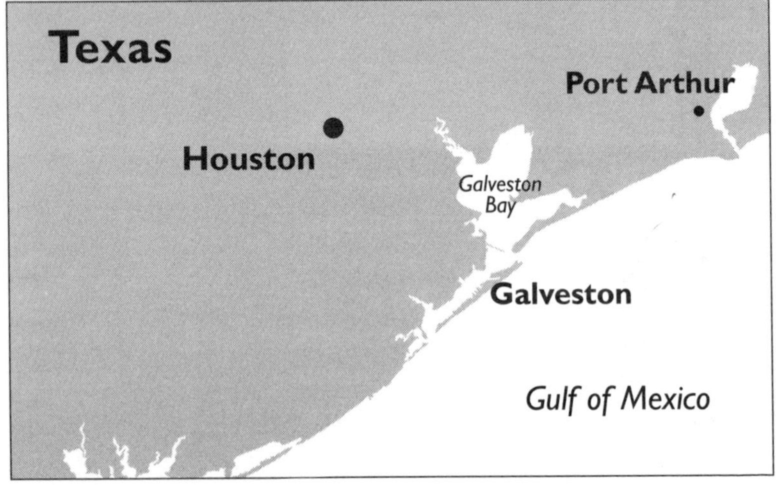
Texas
Port Arthur
Houston
Galveston Bay
Galveston
Gulf of Mexico

CHAPTER 1

"I'm starved," Vernon Long complained to his older sister. "Why can't I have just a bite?"

"You wait for Mama," Dora answered. "She'll be home any minute."

Mama was later than usual. She was working for Mrs. Horner. The Horners lived halfway across town. It was a long walk for Mama.

"You watch out the window," Dora told her brother. "Tell me when you see her coming. Then I'll put the biscuits in the oven."

Dora wasn't quite 14. But she could cook as well as Mama. She'd fixed a big pot of black-eyed peas with bacon rind. And she'd made baking powder biscuits.

There was even a small pat of butter for the biscuits. One of Mama's ladies had given it to her the day before. Mrs. Long did washing, ironing, and cleaning for three or four wealthy families.

Vernon went to the window. He watched for Mama.

"I wish Mama didn't have to work so hard," Vernon said.

"Me too," Dora sighed. "But since Papa—since Papa died—"

Vernon always had a choking feeling when he thought about Papa too. It had been a year since Papa had died. He had worked on the docks. He'd been killed in an accident there. Vernon missed his papa so much.

He missed his baby sister Lena too. Lena had died from yellow fever a few months before Papa was killed.

Vernon had enjoyed playing with his baby sister. She was just learning to walk when she became sick.

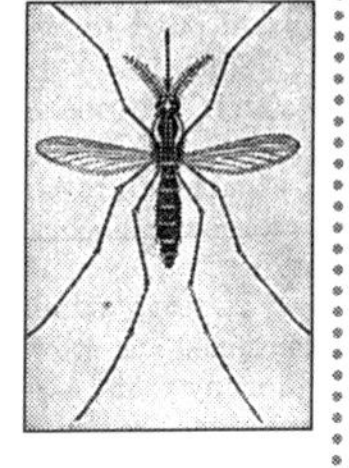

Yellow fever is an infectious disease. It is found in warm, moist areas of the world. The yellow fever virus is carried by a certain type of mosquito.

People with the disease experience high fevers and jaundice, which is a liver problem that turns the skin yellow.

Several yellow fever outbreaks had passed through Galveston in the late 1800s and the early 1900s. At that time, nothing much could be done for those who had the disease.

Sometimes Vernon thought he could still hear the ring of her laughter. He could see her toddling across the room into his outstretched arms.

"Set the table, Vernon," Dora said.

"How can I set the table and watch for Mama at the same time?" Vernon asked.

"Smarty," Dora snapped. She slapped at Vernon.

Vernon dodged her slap and giggled.

"Mama's coming!" Vernon cried. "I can see her." He pushed his nose against the window. "She's carrying a bag of something. It looks heavy."

Dora popped the biscuits into the oven. Vernon dashed out the door.

"I'll go help Mama," he called over his shoulder. "You set the table."

In a few moments, Vernon and Mama reached the cabin. Dora gave her mother a big hug.

"Here's your coffee, Mama," Dora said.

Mama sat down at the table. She groaned as she lifted the cup of steaming coffee. "Mmm," she murmured. "Honey, you do make the best coffee."

Dora beamed. "What's in the bag, Mama?" she asked. "Is it something from Mrs. Horner?"

"You just never mind till after supper," Mama replied.

Dora took the biscuits from the oven. She ladled the black-eyed peas into bowls.

Vernon began to eat noisily.

"Sonny!" Mama scolded. "You tend to your manners."

"I'm too hungry," he said. But he did slow down a little.

After supper, Mama opened the bag. She took out a red plaid shirt.

Some of Mrs. Long's ladies gave her used clothing and other things. Some of the clothes would be in good condition. Nearly all of Dora's and Vernon's school clothes came from Mama's ladies.

"For you," she said to Vernon. "It was young William Horner's. He's just a little bigger than you."

Next she pulled out a pair of pants for Vernon. One knee had a hole.

"I can patch that," said Mama. "They'll be good enough for school."

"What about me, Mama?" Dora asked excitedly. "Their girl, Mildred, is my size. She hardly wears her clothes out."

Mama grinned at her daughter. "Just wait till you see," she said.

There were two dresses, just like new. One was a bright blue **gingham**. The other was a pretty pink one. The pink dress had a small stain on one sleeve.

"A little vinegar water will take that out," Mama told Dora.

A petticoat was also in the bag.

Dora held the dresses against herself. "Oooh!" she squealed. "I can take them with me to Houston. I'll wear the blue one on the train."

Vernon felt his spirits sink. He had almost forgotten. Tomorrow was September 7. In the morning, his sister was going away to Houston. She would be gone for more than three months.

CHAPTER 2

Vernon lay on his straw **pallet** in the **loft**. Below, Mama and Dora slept in the big double bed. Vernon could hear Mama's faint snoring.

Vernon tossed and turned. He thought about the next day. He knew how much he would miss Dora.

Aunt Rachel and Uncle Clem lived in Houston. Aunt Rachel cleaned house for a lady who was going to have a baby soon. The lady wanted to hire a girl to help out for a few months. Aunt Rachel had told her about Dora.

At first, Mama said no. But Dora pleaded. "I'll make a lot of money, Mama. And it's only for a few months. I'll be home for Christmas. I'll send home all the money. Then you won't have to work so hard."

Mama had hugged Dora and cried. "You're a good girl," she'd said. "You're a good, good girl."

Vernon envied Dora because she was going to ride a train. The lady in Houston had sent money for the ticket.

Vernon had never been on a train in his life. He'd never even dreamed of going to Houston.

Dora was almost four years older than Vernon. She had finished the eighth grade. Mama wanted her to go to high school. But Dora said, "We need the money, Mama. It's better if I go to work." So Dora was starting her first job.

Dora had always helped Vernon with his school lessons. Now he'd have to do them alone.

Mama couldn't help Vernon. She had never gone to school. She couldn't even read or write.

Mama fixed a special breakfast. Ham and hotcakes with molasses sat on the table.

Dora's suitcase was all packed. She was wearing her almost-new blue gingham dress. Mama had spent an hour braiding her hair.

Vernon saw Mama wiping away tears. When she saw him watching, she said, "This old stove smokes so bad. It burns my eyes."

But Vernon knew she was sad because Dora was leaving.

A neighbor, Mr. Fisher, was coming around eight o'clock. He was taking Dora to the train **depot**.

Mr. Fisher was an older man who lived two houses from the Longs. He had worked on the docks with Papa. He had retired several years ago.

Mr. Fisher's wife was dead. He had no children nearby. Mama did his washing and sewing sometimes. And he often ate supper with the Longs.

Mr. Fisher came a little early.

"Have a cup of coffee," Mama offered. "Dora will be ready soon."

"I hope to get back as quick as I can," said Mr. Fisher. "Some of those weather fellows are saying we might be in for a storm. I want to get things put away. I'm repairing my henhouse. I have tools and lumber out in the yard."

Vernon glanced out the open door. The wind was blowing pretty hard. It was a warm wind. But Vernon and his family were used to storms. Quite often, Galveston Island was hit with strong winds and high water.

That's why Papa had built the

A storm had been predicted for Friday, September 7, 1900. But many people did not pay much attention. Most storms died before they hit the beach with very much force.

two-room cabin so well. It was high off the ground. All the windows had shutters that closed. Papa had planned to add another room someday.

The cabin was small. But even so, it was warm and cozy. And it was the only home Vernon had ever known.

At last, the moment came for Vernon to tell Dora good-bye. He gave her a hug. She promised to write to him and Mama.

This time, Mama didn't try to hide her tears as Dora left with Mr. Fisher. Vernon watched until the wagon was out of sight.

Mama sniffled and wiped her eyes with her apron. "You get on to school, sonny," she said.

"Do I have to?" Vernon asked. "Why can't I stay home?"

She handed him his lunch. It was a ham sandwich and an apple.

"Get now, sonny," she said. "Don't fuss with me today. I need to hurry to Mrs. Neeley's. I have floors to scrub, windows to wash, clothes to iron, bread to bake—"

Vernon ran out of the cabin and all the way to school.

Vernon had a hard time listening to his teacher, Miss Grove. She was giving a history lesson. History—he hated history. Why couldn't he be as good in school as Dora? Dora loved school.

In his mind, Vernon could see the train chugging along the tracks, carrying Dora all the way to Houston.

CHAPTER 3

Mama was still at work when Vernon arrived home from school. He peeled a cold sweet potato and ate it.

Then Vernon filled the wood box with kindling and wood. He swept the floors and then went outside.

The wind was blowing hard from the north. Vernon walked down the road. The wind whipped at his clothes.

"Hey, Vernon," someone called.

Vernon looked over his shoulder. It was his best friend Luther.

"Let's walk down to the beach," Luther said.

The north wind was much stronger on the beach. The boys sat on a log. They watched the high waves pound against the rocks.

"How high do you think the wind is?" asked Luther.

"Well, it's high," said Vernon. "But not real high. Remember what Miss Grove said? If it blows 74 miles per hour, it's a hurricane."

"I remember," said Luther.

"Hurricanes form over water. Tornadoes form over dry land."

Vernon laughed. "You sound like our teacher. Come on, let's go home."

They walked home in silence. It was so windy that it was hard to talk.

Mama still wasn't home. Vernon sat down at the table. He opened his history book. He started reading out loud. He stumbled over the many big words.

How he wished Dora were home. She was lucky, he thought. She didn't have to go to school anymore.

Vernon had four more years of grade school. Then, he'd go to high school. Vernon didn't want to. He hated school. But he'd promised Papa—a long time ago.

Papa had said, "I don't want you to work on the docks, son. I want you to have a better life."

Vernon knew there wasn't anybody better than Papa. But he'd keep his promise. He'd go to school and make Papa proud.

The cabin was so quiet. Vernon noticed the wind had slowed down a little. That was good.

Vernon tried to think about the weekend. He didn't have school. He could just play with his friends.

When Mama finally came home, Vernon could tell she'd been crying. Her eyes were red and swollen.

Schools in 1900 were segregated. The word *segregated* means "separated." Black students could only go to schools just for blacks. Many towns did not have high schools for black students. Galveston had the first black high school in the state of Texas.

Mama heated up the black-eyed peas. They ate the cold, leftover biscuits. Neither of them talked much during supper. Then they both went to bed early.

CHAPTER 4

Mrs. Long was ready for work when Vernon climbed down from the loft.

"The oatmeal is still hot, son," Mama said. "It's Saturday. So I'll be home by noon. Pick up some **yeast** at the store. I'll bake bread this afternoon."

Vernon rubbed the sleep from his eyes. He yawned.

"Mighty windy this morning," Mama said as she went out the door. It slammed hard behind her.

Vernon carried his bowl of oatmeal to the window. The wind was still blowing from the north.

Things flew through the air. The windows and the door rattled as Vernon finished his breakfast. He washed the dishes.

"Reckon I'd better go get Mama's yeast first thing," he said out loud.

Vernon wondered what Dora was doing as he shut the door behind him. Did she like being in the big city? Did she miss him and Mama?

He really missed Dora. She was always so cheerful. Vernon smiled, thinking how she sang while she worked around the cabin. Sometimes she even danced. That always made him and Mama laugh.

Vernon hunched low against the wind. It was only five blocks to the grocery store. But it took him a long time to get there.

Twice, Vernon dodged slate shingles flying by. He stopped once to help a man catch a barrel that was rolling down the street. They set it upright.

The wind blew very strong from the north on September 8. It blew against the storm that approached from the southeast. In spite of the northerly winds, waves crashed upon the beach with great force. And the tides, which should have been low, kept rising.

Vernon finally reached the store. Several older men were sitting on a bench on the sheltered side. As Vernon drew near, he heard one man say, "I've never seen the tide as high as it is. I wish the city had built the seawall like they planned."

"You know what Isaac Cline said. He said a wall wasn't needed," another man added. "He should know what he's talking about. He's the head weatherman in these parts."

Vernon climbed the steps. He struggled against the wind.

"Howdy, young fellow," said one of the men.

Isaac Monroe Cline was head of the U.S. Weather Service in Galveston in 1900. When the city started making plans to build a seawall, Cline was against the idea. He was sure that Galveston would be safe against any storm. To even think the city would ever be seriously damaged by a hurricane was "an **absurd delusion**" said Cline. The city planners listened to him.

It was Mr. Archer. Vernon had known him all his life. Mr. Archer was a bachelor. Mama did his washing and ironing. Sometimes he hired Vernon to do jobs for him.

Vernon nodded and smiled.

"How's your mama?" asked Mr. Archer.

"She's fine, sir," Vernon answered.

"Mrs. Long is a mighty fine woman," the man said.

Vernon pushed open the heavy store door. Mr. Harvey, the storekeeper, gave Vernon the yeast he asked for.

"How about a peppermint stick, Vernon?" said Mr. Harvey.

"Yes, sir!" Vernon replied. "Thank you!"

Vernon put the yeast into his pocket and started home. He sucked on the peppermint stick.

It was all Vernon could do to walk as he left the store. The wind was very strong. His eyes filled with sand. A fence **picket** hit him on the shoulder. He stumbled and fell.

Mr. Archer came running from the store. He helped Vernon to his feet.

"Are you all right?" he asked the boy.

Vernon rubbed his shoulder.

"I—I think so," Vernon answered. "Yes, I'm fine, thank you."

Mr. Archer patted Vernon on the back. "You'd better get on home fast," he said. "This wind is getting mighty strong."

As Vernon started home, rain began to fall. He dodged flying debris all the way.

Vernon was soaked when he entered the cabin. He pushed the door shut behind him.

Vernon stirred the fire. Then he took off his wet clothes and hung them on a chair near the stove. He put on the clothes Mama had brought home from Mrs. Horner's. He had to roll up the shirt sleeves.

After a while, Vernon warmed up. The roaring of the wind seemed louder. Rain was falling harder. A lilac bush was beating against the side of the cabin.

Vernon wanted to go out and close the storm shutters. But he knew he couldn't do it alone. He was not tall enough.

He wished Mama were home. He worried about her walking in the wind. There was so much debris blowing through the air. He looked at the clock. It was almost eleven. Mama had said she'd be home by noon.

Vernon stood by the window watching for Mama. He thought about

Dora. He wondered if she was homesick. Well, one good thing, Vernon thought, she's missing this awful storm. Dora was scared to death of storms.

Suddenly, Vernon thought he heard another sound besides the wind. It was a human voice. Someone was calling, "Let me in! Let me in!"

Vernon pressed his face against the window. He saw Mr. Fisher struggling up the steps. He was carrying two gunny sacks.

Vernon pulled the door open and the old man stumbled into the cabin. It was several moments before Mr. Fisher could get his breath. He was very upset.

"All my windows blew plumb out," he gasped. "And—and the chickens. They—they were all killed. The henhouse blew down. I didn't get it finished in time."

Vernon felt bad for Mr. Fisher. He poured him a cup of coffee left over from breakfast.

Vernon went back to the window to watch for Mama.

CHAPTER 5

By the time Mama reached home, Mr. Fisher and Vernon had all the storm shutters closed.

Mr. Fisher had brought all the groceries and clothes he could carry. Now he was frying a big skillet of potatoes. Then he cooked eggs to go with the potatoes. Vernon had made a fresh pot of coffee.

Poor Mama. She was breathing so hard she could barely talk. She was shaking all over. Vernon took a quilt from her bed and wrapped it around her.

He held the coffee to her mouth. "Take a swallow, Mama," he coaxed. "It'll warm you up."

Mama's dress had been ripped by the wind. Most of the buttons were gone from her sweater.

"It—it was so—so awful," she stammered. "I fell down over and over. Part of the roof blew off the grocery store. Bessie Rowe's son was injured bad. A very large tree fell on

Mr. Archer's wagon. He—he couldn't bring me home."

Mama took a swallow of coffee. "The tide is so high that it's over the railroad tracks. Mr. Archer said the wind is blowing over 50 miles an hour. I saw two houses blow off their foundations."

Mr. Fisher put dinner on the table. He sat down.

"You don't have to worry about this little house, missus," he said. "Martin did a good job when he built it. He was one fine carpenter, that man."

Vernon felt proud. It was good to hear Mr. Fisher talk about Papa that way.

But Vernon wished Papa were here now. He'd feel a lot safer. He hoped Mama and Mr. Fisher couldn't tell how scared he was. Vernon had seen a lot of storms. But he had never seen one quite like this one.

The fried potatoes and eggs were really good. But Vernon's stomach was so tied in knots he had a hard time swallowing.

Mama had finally stopped shaking.

"You sit right there by the stove," Mr. Fisher said. "I'll wash up these dishes."

By two o'clock in the afternoon, the rain had let up some. But the wind was still blowing hard. The roaring went on and on. Vernon, Mama, and Mr. Fisher had to shout to one another to be heard.

Outside, trees crashed to the ground. Other objects banged against the house.

Vernon wanted to see what was happening. But the windows were all shuttered.

Then Vernon remembered the window in the loft. It was very small.

And it wasn't shuttered. He could see through it.

Vernon climbed the ladder. He lay on his pallet and looked out. Boards, shingles, boxes, and other things flew about. Almost every fence was lying flat on the ground.

The big fir tree in Luther's yard was in the middle of the street. Their front window was broken. Many of their shingles had blown away. Vernon could see Luther and his sister. They were holding up boards for their father to nail over the window. At last, they covered it.

As Vernon watched, he saw at least a foot of water rushing down the street.

Vernon climbed back down the ladder. Mama and Mr. Fisher sat quietly at the table. They seemed to be almost in a trance.

"Mama," Vernon said.

The wind roared, and the cabin creaked.

"Mama," Vernon repeated, louder. "The water's over the street."

Mama took Vernon's hand. She squeezed it.

"We'll be all right, sonny," she said. "We'll be all right."

Vernon could tell Mama was scared. He thought Mr. Fisher was scared too.

Vernon climbed back up to the loft. He looked out the small window. The water was higher. The wind was much stronger. Vernon's heart jumped to his throat as he watched the wind blow over the trees and buildings.

Suddenly, Luther's house was ripped from the ground and splintered to pieces. Vernon cried out, "Luther! Luther!"

He closed his eyes tightly and

sobbed. When he opened his eyes he saw the last of the splintered boards float away.

He pressed his face against the small window. It was getting dark. But he could see someone moving toward the cabin. It was someone he knew. It looked like a woman. She was carrying something. A baby! She was carrying a baby!

In a flash, Vernon was down the ladder.

"Mama! Mama!" he cried. "There's someone coming! A lady with a baby! It looks like Emma Lee."

"Don't go out there!" Mr. Fisher yelled.

But Vernon ran to the door and grabbed the knob. Mr. Fisher was right behind him. As the knob turned, the door flew open. It banged against the wall.

The water was nearly up to the porch. Mrs. Lee was struggling to get up the steps. Mr. Fisher reached out and grabbed her arm.

Her baby, Sarah, was screaming and kicking frantically. Suddenly, she kicked free and fell into the water.

At once, Vernon jumped off the porch into the water. His mother's screams echoed over the roaring of the wind. "No, Vernon! No! No!"

Sarah's mother was screaming also.

Vernon was barely able to grab Sarah's foot. The water tugged at the baby. But Vernon held on tightly.

After what seemed like forever, Mr. Fisher pulled Vernon out of the water. He helped him into the cabin.

Vernon held the screaming baby in his arms. Mrs. Lee took the baby from him.

"You saved my little Sarah," she cried over and over to Vernon. "You saved my baby."

Vernon changed his wet clothes.

"I have something that should fit your Sarah," Mama said to Mrs. Lee.

Vernon saw tears in Mama's eyes when she handed the woman some of baby Lena's clothes.

Mama fixed some warm milk for Mrs. Lee and Sarah.

Mrs. Lee told them her house had been destroyed. Her husband and mother had been killed. "All I have left is my little Sarah," she sobbed.

Outside, the wind blew even harder. The house shook from side to side. But, amazingly, it stood.

Vernon thought about how proud Papa would have been of their little home. "It might not be pretty and it might not be very big. But it's strong," he had boasted.

Sarah finished drinking the warm milk. She began to make chattering sounds. Her mother wiped the milk from her face, then kissed her. Little Sarah began to squirm.

Mrs. Lee put Sarah on the floor. The baby wobbled a little, then stood still. She looked at Vernon. She smiled a big smile. Then, very slowly and wobbly, she took four steps into Vernon's arms.

Vernon choked back a sob as he held her close.

CHAPTER 6

The next day was a beautiful Sunday. It was hard to believe what had happened the day before.

Vernon spent the morning playing with little Sarah. She reminded him so much of his baby sister Lena.

At noon, Mr. Archer came. He made arrangements to take Mr. Fisher to the train depot. He took Emma Lee and Sarah to live with friends.

The little cabin was suddenly very quiet. That is, it was quiet except for Mama's muffled crying.

Vernon ate a piece of bread and jam. He drank some milk.

"I'm going outside, Mama," he said

"No, sonny," Mama answered. "You don't want to see. You don't want to see what happened."

But Vernon did want to see. "I won't be gone long, Mama," he said as he went out the door.

Mama was right. He saw things he didn't want to see. He knew if he went too far from home he might get lost. Nothing looked the same.

Vernon trudged home slowly. Mama was lying on her bed. He could see that she had cried herself to sleep. Vernon fell down across the foot of the bed and slept.

The next morning, Vernon decided to write to Dora. He knew if she had heard of the storm, she would be worried about Mama and him.

September 10, 1900

Dear Sister,

Mama and I hope you are fine. Mama sends her love.

I have something very horrible to tell you. A terrible storm hit Galveston last Saturday. It was the worst thing anyone could imagine. You would not even know our city. Only a few buildings are left standing.

Mr. Archer came yesterday to see how we were. He was surprised that our cabin was hardly damaged. Some of the shingles are gone.

Mr. Fisher's house was destroyed. He stayed with us until Mr. Archer came. Then Mr. Archer took Mr. Fisher to the train depot. Mr. Fisher is going to Arkansas to stay with his son.

Emma Lee and Sarah came to our house after her house blew down. Her husband and mother were killed. Sarah is so cute. Just about the age of our Lena. They are going to live with some folks on the mainland.

Here is the worst thing of all, Dora. My best friend, Luther, and all his family are dead. Their house blew down and washed away. I can't believe I will never see Luther again.

William and Mildred Horner and their father are dead. Mrs. Horner is badly hurt. Their big beautiful house is completely gone. Only part of the fireplace is still standing.

Another sad thing happened. The orphanage was destroyed. All the children but three were killed. So were all the nuns. Mr. Archer said thousands of people were killed in the storm.

Yesterday, I saw the worst thing I have ever seen. I saw a wagon load of dead bodies going through town. The bodies were going to be buried at sea.

I didn't tell Mama about seeing the bodies. I knew it would upset her a lot. She is already very upset. I heard her crying nearly all night. Her good friend, Nellie Baker, was killed.

St. Mary's Orphan Asylum was run by ten Catholic nuns, the Sisters of Charity. Most of the 90 children they cared for had been orphaned when their parents died during the yellow fever epidemics. Only three young boys survived the storm. They had clung to a tree in the water for over a day.

Mayor Jones called a special meeting yesterday. Mr. Archer said it was to choose a relief committee to help take care of the homeless. So many people have no place to go.

The city is going to start rebuilding right away. A seawall is finally going to be built. Then maybe this will never happen again.

Mama and I miss you. Mama says I miss someone to fuss with. But that's not the only reason.

I tell Mama she misses someone to help with the cooking. She just smiles.

I hate to write you this sad letter. But things will be better someday, I think. Aren't you glad Papa was so smart to build such a nice strong house? He kept us safe, even when he wasn't here.

I can hardly wait for Christmas when you will be home.

Signed with love,

Your brother, Vernon

AFTERWORD

Galveston Island lies about 30 miles off the east coast of Texas. This 30-mile-long sandbar is between Galveston Bay and the Gulf of Mexico. The city of Galveston sits on the east end of the island.

Galveston was a rich seaport. More millionaires lived here than in some of the cities in the East. The city was the first in Texas with electricity and phones. The beaches were playgrounds for the rich.

The population of Galveston in 1900 was over 38,000. The death toll was over 6,000 on the island and about 4,000 more on the mainland. The Galveston storm is still considered the worst U.S. natural disaster. Total deaths were more than the 1889 Johnstown flood and the 1906 San Francisco earthquake combined.

During this time, storm-tracking aircraft and satellites didn't exist. The United States Weather Bureau had to rely on reports from sea captains who happened upon the storms. The information was passed from ship to ship until it finally reached land.

The following timeline shows the path of the Galveston storm.

August 27 ....
The storm begins just west of the Cape Verde Islands.

September 4 ....
The storm nears Cuba.

September 5 ....
The storm is now a hurricane. It crosses the Florida Keys.

September 6 ....
The storm turns toward the west.

September 7 ....
The U.S. Weather Bureau in Washington, D.C., notifies Isaac Cline, chief of the Galveston office, that the storm is expected to reach the island.

September 8 Dawn ....
Many go to the beach to watch the ocean crash farther and farther inland.

September 8 10:10 a.m. ....
Cline receives another warning from the U.S. Weather Bureau.

September 8 Noon ....

The wind is blowing 30 miles per hour and increasing. Gulf water stands three to five feet in some streets. Water in Galveston Bay has covered the wagon bridge and train trestles that connect the island to the mainland. Bay water is flooding the north side of the island.

September 8 2:30 p.m. ....
Half of Galveston is underwater.

September 8 4:30 p.m. ....
Bay and gulf water meet, flooding the entire city.

September 8 5:15 p.m. ....
Winds gust to 100 miles per hour.

September 8 6:30 p.m. ....
Water stands 10 feet in the streets. It rises 5 feet in the next hour.

September 8 7:00 p.m. ....
Winds gust to 120 miles per hour.

September 8 7:30 p.m. ....
Winds shift direction. Some estimate gusts at 200 miles per hour.

September 9..........................
The storm is now classified as a tropical storm. It moves up through Oklahoma and Kansas. It is a bright, sunny day in Galveston.

The storm weakened over the next few days. It eventually moved through the Great Lakes, over the St. Lawrence River, and back out to the North Atlantic Ocean.

At the peak of the storm, the seas rose 20 feet higher than normal. The entire island was underwater. All that could be seen were a few elevated houses and tall buildings rising out of the water.

The people of Galveston began at once to rebuild their city after the storm. Within a week, telegraph and water services were restored. By the second week, new telephone lines were installed. Within four weeks, electric trolleys were running once more. Freight was moving again through the harbors. But Galveston would never again be the center of sea trade that it had been.

Two years later, work began on a seawall. It took nearly 60 years to complete it to what it is today. It is 15½ feet above sea level. It protects part of the city that faces the Gulf of Mexico.

Galveston Island is much higher than it was 100 years ago. In some places, the island is as much as 17 feet higher. Buildings and houses were raised on jacks. Then sand was pumped from the shipping channel onto the island. Over 16 million cubic yards of sand were pumped through large pipes. This is enough to fill more than a million dump trucks.

The cost of the seawall and the land raising was more than 3.5 million dollars. That was a tremendous sum in 1900! Since there were no federal programs to cover the damage, most of the money came from the city and the citizens of Galveston.

Glossary

absurd	ridiculous
delusion	false belief
depot	station
gingham	checked cotton fabric
loft	upper room; attic
pallet	mattress that is usually placed on the floor
picket	pointed board that, with others, forms a fence
yeast	ingredient that makes bread rise